Henrietta snorted. "That was a s[...]
would ever pay to see it."

"Yes, they would," snapped Daniel.

"Dad wouldn't. He hates spending money!"

Daniel frowned. Henrietta was right. He shrugged
again. "So what, I'll just ask Mum to give me a cake or
something – I bet she would, because I'm such a
genius!" He smiled at Henrietta, his most annoying
smile, egging her on to start a fight.

But Henrietta ignored him. She had just thought of a
brilliant idea . . .

Henrietta and the Magic Trick is the fifth title in a series of
books about the mischievous Henrietta and her family.

Henrietta

AND THE
MAGIC TRICK

Stan Cullimore
Illustrated by John Farman

YOUNG CORGI BOOKS

HENRIETTA AND THE MAGIC TRICK
A YOUNG CORGI BOOK : 0 552 52829 3

First published in Great Britain by
Piccadilly Press Ltd 1993

PRINTING HISTORY
Young Corgi edition published 1995

Young Corgi Books are published by Transworld Publishers Ltd,
61–63 Uxbridge Road, Ealing, London W5 5SA,
in Australia by Transworld Publishers (Australia) Pty Ltd,
15–25 Helles Avenue, Moorebank, NSW 2170,
and in New Zealand by Transworld Publishers (NZ) Ltd,
3 William Pickering Drive, Albany, Auckland.

Printed and bound in Great Britain by
Cox & Wyman Ltd, Reading, Berkshire.

CONTENTS

STORY ONE

MOTHER'S DAY OFF!

"Mum," Henrietta walked into the living room. "Do you know where my school skirt is?"

Her mother picked up the iron, and sighed. "Yes, I do. It's just about to get ironed."

"Good. It won't take long, will it?"

Before Mum could answer, Daniel strolled into the room looking puzzled. "Has anyone seen my *Computer World*? Only I can't find it."

Mum sighed again. "It's where it

1

should be. In the magazine rack. I put it there when I was tidying up."

Daniel nodded and sat down.

Dad came into the room. "I've lost my book," he said, rather sadly.

"No, you haven't. It's on the mantelpiece — you left it there yesterday!" Mum shook her head. "Honestly, I don't know *what* you lot would do without me. I do all the cleaning, all the cooking, everything. You're hopeless."

Suddenly, she slammed down the iron, and put her hands on her hips. "Hopeless," she repeated.

Dad picked up his book. "Now, that's not entirely true, dear. We do help out sometimes — don't we, kids?"

He smiled at Henrietta and Daniel.

Henrietta and Daniel looked at Mum, then looked at Dad, and did not say a word. They knew something that Dad did not — yet.

Mum was getting angry. She was about to go on the warpath!

Dad turned and smiled at Mum, then saw the dark look on her face. He gulped. "Er . . ."

"Yes," said Mum, between gritted teeth.

Dad laughed nervously. "You're the boss, dear. Would you like *me* to do the ironing?"

Mum nodded. "Yes, thank you, that

would be nice."

"And I'll make you a nice hot cup of tea — shall I, boss?" Daniel stood up.

Mum looked at Henrietta. "And what are you going to do, young lady?"

Henrietta smiled sweetly. "I'm going to give you just what you deserve, Mother."

Mum raised an eyebrow. "And what's that?"

"A day off! Tomorrow, I will be mum. I'll do *all* the cooking, *all* the cleaning, and everything. I like being in charge."

Daniel narrowed his eyes. "I don't trust her. She's up to something. Don't let her do it, Mum."

Mum frowned. "If you don't mind, Daniel, I'm the boss, remember? Now, be quiet." She patted Henrietta on the head.

"Tomorrow," she said, "will be

Mother's Day Off. Henrietta will be in
charge. Won't you, dear?"

The next morning, when Dad came
downstairs to make a cup of tea, he
found Henrietta in the kitchen. She
was wearing Mum's apron.
"What are you doing, Henrietta?"
Henrietta put her hands on her hips,
the way Mum sometimes did. "I might

ask you the same question. What are *you* doing?"

Dad frowned. "But I asked first."

"I don't care. I'm in charge today — remember? It's Mother's Day Off."

Dad nodded. "Oh, yes, so it is."

"So get back up those stairs, now. And *don't* come back down again until you're dressed. Breakfast will be ready in five minutes — do you hear?"

Dad sighed. "You don't half sound like your mother, Henrietta." He went upstairs to get dressed.

Ten minutes later, the family was sitting round the table, eating breakfast, except for Baby-Rose, who was still asleep.

"I don't like this toast. It's burnt," grumbled Daniel.

Henrietta frowned at him. "Well that's your tough luck, isn't it. This isn't a cafe, you know. I've got more things to worry about than you and your toast. I've got a very busy day ahead of me."

Mum and Dad glanced at each other, and tried not to laugh. It was exactly the sort of thing that Mum said to Henrietta whenever *she* complained about the toast being burnt.

"It's not fair," grumbled Daniel. "When can I be mum? I want to be in charge?"

"Well, not just now," snapped Henrietta. "You've got to go upstairs and dress Baby-Rose."

Daniel started to complain.

"Now then, Daniel. Henrietta's in charge — do as you're told," said Dad with a smile.

Henrietta nodded. "And as for you, Dad, you can clear the table and wash the dishes. *I'm* going to bake a cake."

"Oh," said Dad, winking at Mum.

"Ratburgers! I hate washing the dishes."

Half an hour later, Mum came into the kitchen carrying Baby-Rose. "I've just found this young lady in the cupboard, eating sweets. What shall I do with her?"

Henrietta put down the bag of flour

she was holding, and sighed. "Leave her here. I'll look after her." She groaned quietly, the way Mum did whenever *she* was left in the kitchen with Baby-Rose. Then, she went back to measuring out the flour for her cake.

"You won't forget to wash up all those pots and pans you've dirtied — will you?" asked Mum.

"No, of course not. I am in charge, after all."

"And you will remember to tidy up the kitchen when you've finished — won't you?"

Henrietta emptied the flour into a bowl, and picked up an egg. "Stop worrying, mother. Everything's going to be all right. *I'm* in charge now!" She frowned. "Where did I put that butter?"

Just then, Baby-Rose started to giggle. Henrietta looked down at her, and groaned. "Oh no, Baby-Rose! Why did you do that?"

Baby-Rose had found the butter, and had wiped it all over her face.

Mum smiled.

"You're a very silly little baby," muttered Henrietta, picking up her little sister. "Aren't you?"

Baby-Rose did not reply, she had just seen the bowlful of flour. Quickly, she leant over — and tipped it onto the floor.

"BABY-ROSE!" cried Henrietta. "Now look what you've done." She wrinkled her nose. "Aaah, aaah, oh no. Not my sneezy nose!" She tried to stop it. But it was too late. "ATISHOO." She did a Henrietta hyper-sneeze that blew flour, and butter, and egg, all over the kitchen.

Her father came running into the room, followed by Daniel.

"Hahaha," laughed Daniel. "That's a lovely mess you've got to clear up, Henrietta!"

Her father shook his head. "It looks

as if Mum *isn't* going to have a day off, after all."

Henrietta frowned. "What do you

mean? *I'm* in charge, remember. So you just keep quiet. Daniel, you said that you wanted to be mum — well now's your chance. You can look after Baby-Rose. I think she's going to be sick."

"Creep," muttered Daniel.

Dad laughed. "She's got you there, Daniel."

"As for you, Dad," continued Henrietta. "You're always saying that you like helping Mum. Well you can help her now, by tidying the kitchen!"

Dad stopped laughing, and groaned.

"As for you and me, Mum," said Henrietta. "I think we deserve a rest. Come on — let's go and see what's on television."

With that, Henrietta and Mum linked arms, and went into the front room!

STORY TWO

PLAYING IN THE RAIN

DING-DONG!

It was the front doorbell.

"Hello, Lucy," cried Henrietta, opening the front door. "Come in. There's a brilliant film on television."

Lucy was Henrietta's best friend.

Together, the two girls raced into the front room and leapt onto the sofa keeping their shoes on.

Lucy bent down to take hers off.

Henrietta grinned. "Don't bother, Lucy — Mum's not here. She and Baby-

Rose are staying the night at Auntie Annie's."

"Lucky you," said Lucy, dropping the plastic bag she was carrying. She looked at the TV. "What's the film about?"

"Cowboys and Indians," replied Henrietta.

Lucy frowned. "Why are they tying that man to a tree?" she asked.

"Because they're going to do a war dance round him."

"Wow," whispered Lucy. She was quiet for a few moments. "Why have they put that hanky round his mouth?" she asked.

"To keep him quiet."

Lucy opened her mouth to ask another question.

"Shhh," Henrietta put a finger to her lips. "Or else I'll put a hanky round *your* mouth." They both giggled.

14

Henrietta picked up the plastic bag Lucy had brought in with her. "What's this, Lucy?"

"Just a rubbish magazine that my brother asked me to give to Daniel, that's all."

Henrietta smiled. "If it's rubbish, I think we should put it in the bin. Don't you?" She dropped the bag into the bin, and smiled her cheekiest smile.

Just then, the door to the front room opened, and Henrietta's father walked in. He looked at the television and shook his head. "You watch too much television, young lady. It's not good for you."

He switched it off, and then noticed Lucy.

"Now then, Lucy," he said. "Surely you didn't come round to play with Henrietta, just to spend all day in the house watching television, did you?"

Lucy was just about to say that actually she *did* come round to spend all day in the house watching television, when she caught Henrietta's eye.

Henrietta was shaking her head. She could feel one of her father's lectures coming on.

"Oh no," said Lucy sweetly. "I don't really like watching television at all."

16

Henrietta gave her a thumbs up.

But it was too late. Her father had already started giving his usual lecture, about how *Unhealthy* it was to *Watch Television*. And how *Healthy* it was to *Play Outside*.

When he had finished, Dad went upstairs to phone Auntie Annie's, to find out what time Mum was coming home with Baby-Rose.

The girls went out to the garden.

"Ratburgers," groaned Henrietta when they got there. "No more television for us. We've got to *Play Outside* and get *Healthy*." She started to do an imitation of her father giving a lecture. Lucy giggled.

"I'll tell on you," said her sensible brother Daniel, who had heard Dad's lecture several times before.

"What for?" asked Henrietta.

"Making fun of Dad," replied Daniel, raking up some leaves that had fallen onto the lawn.

"You wouldn't."

"Oh, yes I would."

Henrietta turned to Lucy and pulled a face. "See what a creep my little brother is?"

"I am *not* a creep!" snapped Daniel. "It's just that Dad's right. It's much more *Healthy* to *Play Outdoors*. Watching television is bad for you. Everyone knows that." He sighed and turned to Lucy.

"Lucy," he said sweetly. "Do you have a computer magazine for me? From your brother?"

Lucy nodded. Henrietta giggled.

"It's in the front room." She nudged Lucy. "Isn't it, Lucy?" Lucy nodded again, then also started to giggle.

Daniel sighed. "Girls!" He put down

18

the rake, and went into the house.

"Come on, Lucy," said Henrietta, after Daniel had gone. "Let's have a game of Cowboys and Indians. You can be the Cowboy."

"But I don't want to be the Cowboy,"

moaned Lucy.

"Nor do I." Henrietta thought for a moment.

"Someone's got to be the Cowboy or else we can't play. But who?"

Just then, Daniel came back out of the house. "I can't find my magazine anywhere. Where abouts is it?"

Henrietta smiled, and then winked at Lucy. "I think we've just found our Cowboy!"

Five minutes later, Daniel was tied to the apple tree at the bottom of the garden, looking worried.

"You will let me go, won't you, Henrietta?"

Henrietta nodded. "Of course we will, Daniel. As soon as we've finished playing our game."

"Then you *will* tell me where the computer magazine is, won't you."

"Of *course* we will, Daniel. Now relax — and remember, you mustn't talk until I tell you to. Or else I'll put a hanky round your mouth."

With that, she and Lucy went back into the house to look for Indian clothes. They were going to dress up.

Five minutes later, when Henrietta and Lucy walked into the kitchen, they found Dad frowning at the sky.

"I'm sorry, girls," he said. "You can't go outside just now, it's raining."

"But you told us to play outside," moaned Henrietta. "We're playing a game with Daniel."

"Well you'll just have to play it indoors, I'm afraid." Dad looked around. "Talking of Daniel. Where is he? I haven't seen him for ages."

Henrietta gulped. "Daniel? Er . . . he's outside."

"Where?"

"At the bottom of the garden."

Dad looked out of the window. "But he'll be soaked. Why doesn't he come in?"

Henrietta smiled nervously. "Because we tied him to a tree."

Dad gasped. "You did what?"

"We tied him to a tree."

"Well you can just go outside and *un*-tie him then, can't you?" Dad shook his head. "Honestly, Henrietta — sometimes you do the strangest things."

He watched in disbelief as Henrietta and Lucy ran out of the door and into the pouring rain.

Two minutes later, they were back again, soaking wet.

"Where's Daniel?" asked Dad.

Henrietta looked embarrassed. "We can't undo the knots, Dad. He's stuck!"

Lucy nodded. "She's right. We can't undo the knots."

Dad sighed, "This is ridiculous."

Then, he followed the girls as they ran
back down the garden path, to where
Daniel was waiting.

By the time they reached the tree,
they were *all* soaked to the skin.

"Sometimes," said Dad, as he
wrestled with the soggy rope that was
tied around Daniel's waist, "I wonder
where I went wrong with you children."

The rope fell to the floor, and landed in a puddle.

"I mean, I'm not surprised by Henrietta — she's always doing daft things. But why on earth you *let* them tie you to a tree, I'll never know, Daniel."

"We were playing a game," muttered Henrietta, shivering. "Like you told us to. Weren't we, Daniel?"

But Daniel did not reply.

He was too cold, too wet, and too miserable to care.

The next morning, when Henrietta's mother came home, Henrietta and Daniel were lying in bed, with streaming colds.

Daniel was reading his new computer magazine.

"Whatever have you been up to?" asked Mum, sitting on Henrietta's bed.

"You've all got colds, even Lucy. Her mother's just phoned."

"We were playing outdoors," croaked Henrietta.

"In all that rain?" asked Mum. "Why?"

Henrietta sniffed. "Because Dad told us to."

Her mother sighed. "Did he give you his usual lecture about how *Unhealthy* television is?"

Henrietta nodded.

Mum shook her head. "The next time Lucy comes round, I think you should both stay in the house and watch television."

"Why?" asked Henrietta.

Mum smiled. "It's more *Healthy*!"

STORY THREE

THE KITE CUP

"Evening all!" Dad walked into the breakfast room, and smiled at his family as they sat eating their lunch.

There was no reply.

Dad coughed. "I said: 'evening all!'"

Mum looked up. "I am *not* in a good mood."

"Oh," said Dad, putting down the long brown parcel he was holding. "Why not?"

"Ask your children."

Dad turned to Daniel. "Why isn't your mother in a good mood, son?"

Daniel put down the knife and fork he was holding, and stood up. "Because Henrietta broke Mum's Jubilee eggcup, that's why." He sat down.

"No, I didn't," cried Henrietta, swallowing the rest of her green banana in one gulp. "It was you."

"No, it wasn't!"

"Yes, it was!"

Dad held up his hands for silence. For once, it worked. "Do I take it that Mum's favourite eggcup has just been broken?"

Henrietta and Daniel nodded.

"Has anyone said 'Sorry', to Mum?"

After a moment, Henrietta and Daniel shook their heads.

"Then I think that someone *should* say it. Don't you?" said Dad.

"Sorry, Mum," said Henrietta and

Daniel quietly.

Mum snorted. She was still upset.

Dad went and stood behind her, and put his arm on her shoulder. "I think what you need," he said, "is a rest from these troublesome children, who have been stuck at home all day. Am I right?"

Mum nodded.

"Well, the good news is that after lunch I'm taking them all up to The

Downs. So you'll get a nice rest. How does that sound?"

Mum sighed. "Perfect!"

"Any questions?" asked Dad.

"Yes," said Henrietta. "What's inside that long brown parcel?"

Dad smiled. "Our new kite."

"Yippee," cried Henrietta. "I love kites."

"I don't know why," muttered Daniel. "I'm much better at flying them than you are."

After they had finished lunch — and doing the washing up, Dad, Daniel, Henrietta and Baby-Rose set off for The Downs to fly the new kite.

"Now," said Dad as they walked along, "before we do anything else, I want to know what you two . . ." He peered at Daniel and Henrietta over the top of his glasses "are going to do about Mum's eggcup — she'd had it for years. And she was very fond of it."

"There's only one thing we can do," said Daniel in his most sensible, grown-up voice. "We shall have to buy her another."

"Ratburgers," grumbled Henrietta. "I was saving up to get myself a new pair of slippers."

"Well, I was saving up for a book," snapped Daniel. "But it can't be helped. We *must* get Mum a new eggcup."

"Creep," muttered Henrietta.

Dad smiled. "I'm proud of you, Daniel. That's exactly what I think you should do."

"What about me? Aren't you proud of me?" squawked Henrietta. "I'm going to buy her a new eggcup as well, you know."

"I'm proud of you both," said Dad.

"Come on, I'll race you to the corner."

When they got to The Downs, they all helped unpack the new kite, apart from Baby-Rose, who was too busy blowing dandelion clocks.

"Dad," said Henrietta, "why did you buy a new kite? You're too old to fly kites."

Dad laughed. "No, I'm not. Anyway, there's a Kite Flying Competition up here tomorrow. And I thought that maybe you or Daniel might want to enter it. Do you?"

"Yes, please," shouted Henrietta and Daniel together.

"Good," said Dad. "Now, Daniel. You can hold the kite, while Henrietta unwinds the string. All right?"

Henrietta nodded.

Daniel whistled. "Amazing! Henrietta is *actually* being helpful for once." Henrietta grinned.

"Of course I am. If you hold the kite and I hold the string, I get first go at flying the kite." She sighed. "You're so *stupid* sometimes, Daniel."

When they got home, Mum was in a better mood.

"How was the new kite?" she asked.

"Brilliant," cried Henrietta. "I was better at flying it than Daniel. So I'm going to win the competition. Yippee!"

She began dancing around the room.

"Actually," said her sensible brother Daniel, "I rather think that I was better at flying it than Henrietta was. And I'm sure that the judges tomorrow will agree with me."

Dad coughed. "There's one slight problem with that."

Henrietta stopped dancing. "What?"

"I've only got *one* entry form — so only one of you can enter the competition tomorrow. Sorry."

Mum smiled. "It's obvious. They should enter the competition together, as a team."

Henrietta pulled a face, and even Daniel looked as if the very idea made him feel sick.

But it was no good.

Mum and Dad had made up their minds.

The next day, Mum stayed at home while Dad took Henrietta and Daniel to the Kite Flying Competition.

"Oh, dear," said Dad when they got there. "It doesn't look very hopeful, does it?" There was hardly any wind. They watched as a few of the entrants tried to make their kites fly, and failed.

"This is rubbish," grumbled Henrietta, as she pulled out her handkerchief and wiped her nose. "It's freezing cold. There's not enough wind, and I'm stuck in a team with Stupid Old Daniel!"

She wiped her nose again, and waited impatiently.

Eventually, a voice came over the loudspeaker. "Entry number 37. Henrietta and Daniel — where are you please?"

"Come on, it's your turn," said Dad. He helped Henrietta and Daniel set up the kite and carry it into The Flying Zone.

"I'll fly it first," said Daniel. "Then you can have a go, Henrietta."

Dad launched the kite, and stood back. There was a tiny burst of wind, and it flew into the sky. But then the wind died again and the kite started to sink slowly to the ground.

"You see, you're rubbish. Give me a go!" Henrietta grabbed at the string — and missed. She fell headfirst into the long grass.

"Hahaha. Serves you right," laughed Daniel.

"Shut up," snapped Henrietta. "Now look what you've done, you've made my nose go all aah . . ., all aah . . ., oh no," she tried to stop it. "Not my sneezy nose!" But it was too late.

"ATISHOO." She did a Henrietta
hyper-sneeze that blew the kite high
into the sky, and made it dance — and
jiggle, and whirl.

"Fantastic!" cried the voice over the
loudspeaker. "That's the last entry, and

clearly they *have* to win the
competition. Henrietta and Daniel,
please come this way, so I can award
you first prize. The Kite Cup!"

Daniel and Henrietta proudly went
up to receive their prize.

But as they took it back to Dad, they
looked anything *but* proud. The Kite
Cup was tiny!

"It looks more like an *egg* cup to me,"
laughed Dad when he saw it.

Slowly, Henrietta and Daniel
exchanged glances. They smiled. They
had *both*, just had a brilliant idea.

When they got home, Mum was
waiting for them.

"How did it go?" she asked.

"Well," said Henrietta. "The *good*
news is that we won first prize." She
giggled, excitedly.

"Congratulations," said Mum.

"The *bad* news," said Daniel, "is that there was only *one* prize — and we can't share it." He pretended to be annoyed.

"Oh, dear. That is a pity, isn't it?" said Mum.

"Not really," said Daniel, "because

we've decided to give it to *you*!"

"Because we really *are* sorry that we broke your eggcup, Mum," said Henrietta. "Aren't we, Daniel?"

Daniel nodded.

"So we want you to have this."

Henrietta handed her mother a small cardboard box.

Mum opened it, and took out a tiny silver cup, just like an eggcup. Around the outside of it were written the words: THE KITE CUP.

Mum blinked. "Oh dear!"

"What's wrong, Mum? Don't you like it?" asked Henrietta anxiously.

Her mother shook her head. "It's not that."

"Then what is it?" asked Daniel.

Mum sniffed. "I think I'm going to cry."

And then, she did.

STORY FOUR

THE MAGIC SET

Henrietta was bored.

She went into the kitchen.

"Mum, can I have something to eat? I'm starving." She reached out to pick up a green iced doughnut that was sitting on a plate by the breadbin.

Her mother tapped her on the hand. "No, you cannot have anything to eat, young lady. And leave that doughnut alone — it's your father's!"

"Ratburgers," muttered Henrietta.

"Are you bored?" asked her mother.

"Yes!"

"Well, why don't you go into the front room and see Daniel — he's playing with his new magic set. I'm sure he'll need help with some of the magic tricks."

"BOR-ING!"

"Well, in that case, there's a little job you can do for me . . ."

Henrietta groaned. She hated doing 'little jobs' for Mum. They were always *really* boring. Suddenly, she had an idea.

"It's all right, Mum. I'm not bored any more. I'm going to help Daniel practise his magic tricks." She walked out of the kitchen, and sighed. "Phew, what a lucky escape. I hate being helpful." She grinned, and rubbed her hands together.

"Now to go and annoy Daniel!"

When she got to the front room, she found Daniel wearing his magician's hat and reading his *Book of Magic* which he held in one hand. In the other hand he was holding his magic wand. He looked up.

"Hello, Henrietta. Can you come over here and help me do this trick?"

Henrietta groaned. "Everyone wants me to *help* them today. I *hate* being helpful."

"Please, Henrietta. You have to help me do this trick. It's really easy." Daniel sniggered. "In fact, it's so easy — even you could do it!"

"Shut up!" snapped Henrietta.

"Watch," said Daniel. He took his handkerchief out of his pocket, and placed it on the coffee table. Then, he covered it with his magician's hat, and waved his magic wand.

"What's so good about that?"

Daniel smiled his most magical smile. "I can now remove the hanky from underneath the hat — without touching the hat!"

"Rubbish," snorted Henrietta.

Daniel folded his arms and did not say a word.

Henrietta frowned. "I don't believe you."

Daniel shrugged. "If you don't believe me, why don't you have a look?"

"All right then, I will." Henrietta leant down and slowly lifted up the hat, to look beneath it. Quick as a flash, Daniel grabbed his handkerchief and held it up.

"There! I *told* you I could remove the hanky without touching the hat. And I did, so there. Ha!"

Henrietta scowled.

"I'm such a brilliant magician," continued Daniel. "When I've finished practising all my other tricks, I shall put on a show for Mum and Dad. *And*, I shall charge them money to get in."

Henrietta snorted. "That was a stupid trick. No-one would ever pay to see it."

"Yes, they would," snapped Daniel.

"Dad wouldn't. He hates spending money!"

Daniel frowned, Henrietta was right.

He shrugged again. "So what, I'll just ask Mum to give me a cake or something — I bet she would, because I'm such a genius!" He smiled at Henrietta, his most annoying smile, egging her on to start a fight.

But Henrietta ignored him.

She had just thought of a brilliant idea. She licked her lips, and thought of doughnuts. Then, while Daniel went

back to his book, she picked up his
magician's hat and his magic wand, and
tiptoed out of the room.

In the kitchen, Dad was sitting at the
table drinking a cup of tea. In front of
him was his green iced doughnut. He
blew some sawdust from his fingers,
and picked up the cake.

"STOP," shouted Henrietta, running
into the room. "Don't eat that
doughnut!"

Her father frowned. "Why not? I've
just finished sawing a whole load of
wood — and I'm starving. Why can't I
eat my doughnut?"

Henrietta smiled, what she hoped
was a mysterious smile. "Because it's a
magic doughnut!"

Dad put his doughnut back on the
plate, and looked at it closely. "Doesn't
look very magical to me," he said.

"Well it is. If I put this magician's hat over it . . ." Henrietta placed the hat over the doughnut, ". . . and then tap the hat with this magic wand . . ." Henrietta tapped the hat with the wand, ". . . I can do a magic trick."

"What sort of magic trick?" asked Dad.

"A very clever one," replied Henrietta. "I can remove the doughnut from underneath the hat — without touching the hat."

"Really," said Dad.

"Yes," said Henrietta.

At that moment Daniel walked into the kitchen. "Give me back my magician's hat, Henrietta, and my magic wand. I didn't say you could borrow them — did I? I want to do my magic show for Mum and Dad."

"In a minute," hissed Henrietta. "I'm just doing a magic trick. Aren't I, Dad?"

Dad nodded. "Henrietta is going to remove my doughnut from under the hat — without touching it."

Daniel narrowed his eyes. "That's *my* trick," he said between gritted teeth. "And she's stolen it."

Henrietta ignored him.

Daniel's face went red, as he got more and more angry. Finally he snapped. "I can prove it's my trick. I know what she's going to do. She's going to wait until you pick up the hat,

49

and then grab the doughnut!"

"That's not fair! You're not allowed to tell him." Henrietta stamped her foot. "I hate you, Daniel!"

Dad frowned. "Now then, Henrietta. That's *not* a very nice thing to say. I already *knew* what you were going to do — I've seen it done before." He patted her on the head. "Never mind."

Some sawdust fell onto Henrietta's nose.

"Aaah, aaah. Oh no, not my sneezy nose." She tried to stop it. But it was too late. She did a Henrietta hyper-sneeze which blew the magician's hat high into the air.

Quick as a flash, Henrietta grabbed the plate with the green iced doughnut on it. "There, how's *that* for a magic trick?"

"Rubbish," muttered Daniel, who was still annoyed.

Dad laughed. "That's very good, Henrietta! But how about this?" He reached out, picked up the doughnut — and swallowed it in one gulp.

"Hey, that's not fair," cried Henrietta. "I did the magic trick, I should get the doughnut!"

Her mother, who had been watching all the time, burst out laughing. "You didn't need to do any magic to get a doughnut, Henrietta. That's the 'little job' I wanted you to do, to run round to the corner shop and get *two*

doughnuts for you and Daniel."

She reached for her purse. "It would have saved a lot of time if you had listened to me in the first place."

"Oh, I don't know," replied Henrietta. "I've learnt a really clever new trick."

"Yes, and I taught it to you," snorted Daniel.

"Oh, I wasn't thinking of *your* trick, Daniel," replied Henrietta cheekily. "I was thinking of *Dad's* trick."

Shortly afterwards, while Daniel did his magic show for Mum and Dad, Henrietta opened the front door and set off for the corner shop.

She smiled to herself as she skipped down the street. Then she started to giggle. "I wonder if I can make *both* doughnuts disappear before I get home . . ."

HENRIETTA AND THE TOOTH FAIRY

Stan Cullimore

"Oh no. Not my sneezy nose." Henrietta tried to stop it. But it was too late . . .

Henrietta is always being naughty. She doesn't *want* to be like her sensible brother Daniel. And her sneezy nose keeps making her sneeze at all the wrong moments – at the swimming pool, buying new shoes, or trying to do good deeds. When Henrietta gets a wobbly tooth, she wants it to fall out quickly so that the tooth fairy will come. But things don't work out quite as Henrietta plans . . .

A delightful series of four stories about the mischievous Henrietta and her family – ideal for beginner readers.

"Children responded well to this lively, active book which has plenty of drawings to sustain their interest" *Federation of Children's Book Groups, Pick of the Year*

0 552 52745 9

YOUNG CORGI BOOKS

HENRIETTA'S BUBBLE TROUBLE

Stan Cullimore

"Yippee," Henrietta cried, as she pushed her rubber duck under the water. "I love bubbles."

Henrietta and her sensible brother, Daniel, are being given a real treat, but first she must have a bath without making any mess. That's not easy to do when you're Henrietta! Once again her sneezy nose looks as if it will land her in trouble, or will it?

A lively collection of four stories about the mischievous Henrietta and her family.

0 552 52746 7

YOUNG CORGI BOOKS

HENRIETTA AND THE GHOST CHASE

Stan Cullimore

"GHOSTS! They're after me. HELP! They've come to chase me away."

It's a boring Sunday afternoon for Henrietta and to make it worse her sensible brother, Daniel, won't let her play his *Ghost Chase* game on the computer.

But, with the help of her sneezy nose, Henrietta discovers her own version of the game which leaves Daniel wondering if ghosts are as much fun as he thought!

A lively collection of four stories about the mischievous Henrietta and her family – ideal for beginner readers.

0 552 52747 5

YOUNG CORGI BOOKS

HENRIETTA'S POCKET MONEY

Stan Cullimore

"Ratburgers! I haven't got any money."

Henrietta is *very* cross. She really wants this week's edition of *Hippo Fun*, but she doesn't have any pocket money left. Even worse, her sensible brother Daniel won't stop boasting about how much money *he's* managed to save. Luckily, with the help of her sneezy nose, Henrietta discovers a sneaky way of getting exactly what she wants!

A fun-filled collection of four stories about the mischievous Henrietta and her family – ideal for beginner readers.

0 552 52828 5

YOUNG CORGI BOOKS